Dangerous Giants
Island

Rockand
Ahardplace Sea

Cranky Giant
Continent

Yelling Bay

Village of Nohope

Spit Islands

Island of
Giants in Love

Juuochin Sea

YYYZ Sea

The Cloud Continent

Needanax
Inlet

Littletoun

Beanstalk Bay

"THERE WERE GIANTS IN
THE EARTH IN THOSE DAYS."

— Genesis, chapter 6, verse 4

To Anthony, who had the idea;
to Emily, who would not give up;
and to Kevin, who made a giant's dream
a reality. —W. M. M.

Text copyright © 2005 by Walter M. Mayes
Illustrations copyright © 2005 by Kevin O'Malley

First published in the United States of America in 2005 by
Walker Publishing Company, Inc.
Distributed to the trade by Holtzbrinck Publishers

For information about permission to reproduce selections from
this book, write to Permissions, Walker & Company,
104 Fifth Avenue, New York, New York 10011.

Library of Congress Cataloging-in-Publication Data available upon request
ISBN 0-8027-8974-9 (hardcover)
ISBN-13 978-0-8027-8974-7 (hardcover)
ISBN 0-8027-8975-7 (reinforced)
ISBN-13 978-0-8027-8975-4 (reinforced)

Book design by Shoot the Moon

Visit Walker & Company's Web site at www.walkeryoungreaders.com

Printed in Hong Kong

10 9 8 7 6 5 4 3 2 1

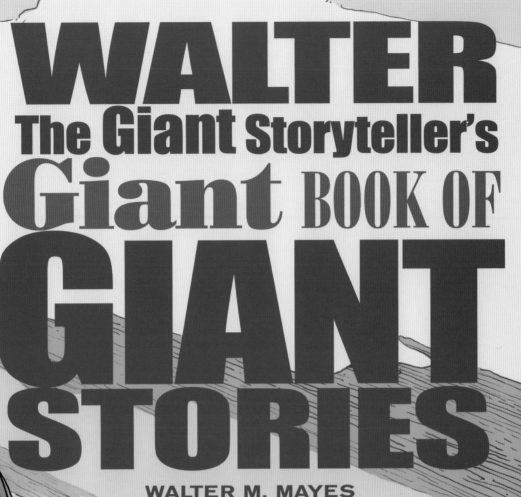

WALTER
The Giant Storyteller's
Giant BOOK OF
GIANT STORIES

WALTER M. MAYES

ILLUSTRATIONS BY KEVIN O'MALLEY

I could remember the last wave as it crashed over the stern of my ship, the roar of the wind and the sound of the splintering wood as we sank. Then I must have blacked out. When I awoke, I was startled to find that, no matter how I struggled, I could only move my head.

I heard tiny feet running and voices. I looked toward the sound and saw a line of people approaching, all carrying torches or weapons. When they marched right up to me, I wished I could rub my eyes, as my vision was surely playing tricks on me!

These people were no bigger than my head.

One stepped forward and spoke in a surprisingly deep voice: "O Evil Giant! I am Magnus, ruler of this island. For the past day and night, your rampage has terrorized our people. Livestock have run off, dwellings have been flattened, and we have lived in fear of being captured and devoured. We tied you down while you slept so that you cannot harm us further."

"Wait a minute!" I cried out, and everyone stepped back. "First of all, I am not evil! Giants aren't evil. And second, if you'll just let me up, I think I can put an end to your prob—"

Before I could finish, my accuser stepped forward again.

"For centuries, giants have roamed the earth, destroying villages and lives. They are mean, vicious, stupid, and clumsy, killing people by accident as well as on purpose. We will be your victims no longer. You are ordered to stand trial for the crimes of giants. If found guilty, you will be put to death."

"Now hold on!" I shouted. Then I realized that yelling was only making me look scarier, so I quieted down. "I would never hurt anyone. I'm not that kind of a giant. I'm a storyteller—one of the good guys."

Magnus continued. "Then you should know that the stories of the world's greatest heroes highlight their triumphs over frightening giants."

David defeating Goliath . . .

Gilgamesh decapitating Huwawa, the giant guardian of the cedar forest . . .

The Navaho warrior gods Nayenezgani and Tobadzistsini beheading a giant who threw four hundred thunderbolts at them . . .

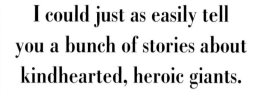

I could just as easily tell you a bunch of stories about kindhearted, heroic giants.

The Giant of Grabbist, who saved a fishing boat crew from a raging storm . . .

Annie Christmas, a free woman of color who could pole up the Mississippi even faster than Mike Fink . . .

Ysbaddeden, King of the Giants, whose fairness as a ruler was exceeded only by his love of his daughter . . .

But stories about bad giants sell more newspapers, if you know what I mean. So nobody hears much about the brave and helpful giants.

This seemed to have little effect on the crowd. I had to think fast.

"If I am on trial here, don't I get to defend myself?" I asked.

There was some discussion, and then Magnus turned to me and said, "What do you offer as your defense?"

"Why, stories, of course! Look, most giants just try to get along in a world much too small for them, but what do they get for their efforts? Slaughtered! Then, to add insult to injury, they become fodder for some so-called hero's bragging. You know that history is just the stories told by the winners, right?"

Some little heads nodded at this.

"You're probably familiar with Jack and the Beanstalk, eh? Because of that story you think I'm going to say 'FEE-FI-FIDDLE-DEE-FOO' and eat you, right? Well, I don't eat people, and no one in my family does, either. No story has done more damage to the reputation of giants than that one. The version you've heard is so wrong. That little weasel Jack got away with murder—literally!"

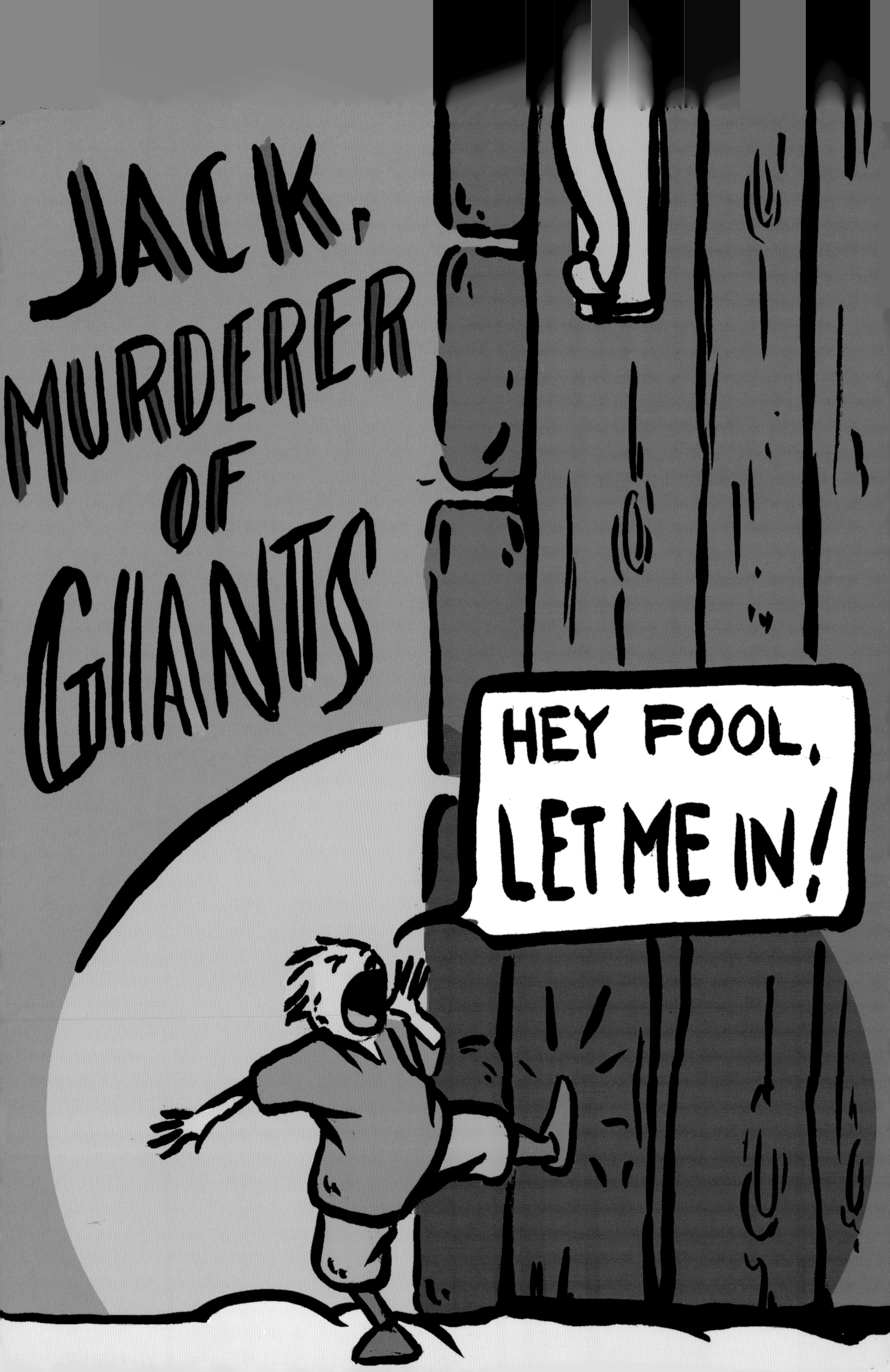
JACK, MURDERER OF GIANTS
HEY FOOL, LET ME IN!

Jack was a thievin', lazy boy who lived with his long-suffering mother. You know the story: There was a cow that didn't give milk and had to be sold and Jack wound up with five beans instead of money, but the beans turned out to be magic and a beanstalk grew, right?

Well, that's mostly true, but when he climbed the beanstalk and found a great castle looming in the distance, Jack ran toward it, hoping for something to steal. Reaching the gate, he found it to be so enormous that he could easily slip between the bars. A huge entryway revealed a door with light and music coming from it,

He entered an enormous kitchen. Yes, there was a golden harp, a kindly giantess, and a goose that laid golden eggs, but that's only the half of it.

This was no adventure story I'm talkin' about, and Jack was no hero—this was a home invasion, and Jack was a punk! What kind of a hero triumphs by cheating?

Jack walked right in and romanced a man's kindhearted wife, tricking her so he could make repeated visits and take things that weren't his. Then, to top it all off, he murdered the owner of the house!

"The giant found Jack stealing his things and ran after him to get them back. Jack chopped down the beanstalk knowing full well that the giant was climbing down. It was cold-blooded murder!"

"There would have been a rampage," Magnus continued, "if the giant came down and started smashing houses. Jack was protecting his home and the whole village."

I could not let this stand. "No way! Giants go out of their way to avoid stepping on people smaller than themselves—and their houses! Where I come from, most of the giant stories are about giants helping people."

I had an idea.

"Ever heard of a Tall Tale?" I asked.

"Of course," Magnus replied. "I know more about your culture than you think."

"Then you know that every country has its own storytelling tradition, and the Tall Tale is America's. People told these tales of the heroic exploits and gigantic feats of the men and women who helped the regular-sized folk build the big country that became the good old U.S. of A. Sure, some things got exaggerated along the way, as people traveled and the stories got retold, but at the heart of every Tall Tale there lies a truth.

"You know the most popular heroes of the American Tall Tale: Johnny Appleseed, John Henry, Slue-foot Sue, Mike Fink. But I'll bet that when you think Tall Tales, one name comes immediately to mind, and it's the name of one of the greatest giants ever: Paul Bunyan!"

Magnus's eyes glowed with smugness. "Paul Bunyan's made up. I happen to know that he was created by a lumber company. He's just a commercial grown out of control!"

I had him right where I wanted him. "Oh, he's real, all right. He has helped too many people through the years for anyone to deny his existence! And I'll prove it." I lifted my head, looked at the crowd and announced: "I'd like to call a witness."

John Henry   **Mike Fink**

Slue-foot Sue   **Johnny Appleseed**

The crowd gasped as the world's most famous lumberjack came striding through the trees, his ax over his shoulder. Crouching in a safe spot, away from any of the little people, Paul took off his cap, and said, "How can I help?" His gentle respect for the little people's world and size was obvious.

"How about a little help with these ropes, Paul?" I called. "I'm mighty uncomfortable."

With one swing of his ax, he cut some of the ropes so I could sit up.

"Thank you for coming, Paul," I said as I rubbed my arms, trying to get the blood flowing again. "I was hoping you could tell us a story about one of your big friends to help my judge and jury here to understand that we giants aren't a threat to them."

"Well," said Paul, "you're the storyteller. But I'll be happy to do what I can. D'ya think they'd like to hear about Ol' Stormalong?"

"A perfect choice, Paul. Go ahead."

Stormalong

AS TOLD BY PAUL BUNYAN

Alfred Bulltop Stormalong was his name, but I, like everybody else, just called him Stormy. He was the biggest and the best sailin' man that ever lived, and I know a lot about bein' the biggest and the best at somethin'. He stood sixteen feet high, ate a side of shark and a dozen ostrich eggs for breakfast, and wrestled a giant Kraken single-handed. And he beat it, too! Tied its eight arms into knots!

Stormy's was the tallest ship in the sea, a clipper ship so enormous it required no less of a man than myself to chop down wood enough to build it!

The *Courser* she was called, and Stormy captained her crew of six hundred men and a fleet of horses needed to help officers get from stem to stern. It took forty seamen to handle her pilot's wheel, though Stormy could do it with his little finger. Her rigging was so tall that it pierced the clouds, and clean-shaven young men who climbed to the crow's nest grew a full beard by the time they came down. Her sails were so vast they were made in the only open space large enough to hold them: the Sahara desert! She was so big that she stayed permanently at sea because no harbor was big enough to allow her to turn around.

Durin' the War of 1812, around the time I was clearin' the North Woods,
Stormy and his crew were made honorary members of the United States Navy.
They spent their days lookin' up 'n' down the Atlantic for British warships.
Near the cliffs at Dover, they'd caught sight of a small fleet headin' for
American waters and set off in full pursuit when the *Courser* was blindsided
by as nasty a nor'easter as ever seen.

Stormy ordered the men to batten down the hatches and stay below while he
held onto the wheel. For hours the wind blew and the storm raged.

Now, Stormy knew the strait between Dover and Calais was simply not
wide enough for safe passage, but he had a brilliant idea. He had all the ship's
soap brought on deck.

"We'll swab her sides! That'll make her as slippery as an eel."

When both sides of the *Courser* were caked six inches thick with white soap, Stormy eased her through the narrow passage.

Those cliffs at Dover scraped off every last bit of that soap, but the *Courser* made it through. To this day, they're called the White Cliffs of Dover, all because of Stormy. Y'can still see foam from the soapsuds in the channel below. Take a look sometime if y'don't believe me!

Even with the delay from the storm and all, the *Courser* and her crew made it back across the Atlantic in the nick o' time! The biggest battle of the war was ragin', and it looked none too good for the Americans until Stormy and his men showed up. With their help, the war was won, the British were sent packin', and our new nation continued to grow, independent and proud.

"Howz'at?" asked Paul, clearly pleased with his efforts.

"Wonderful. Thank you very much, Paul," I said. "Your witness, Magnus."

"The reckless damage done to the cliffs at Dover sounds like environmental sabotage to me," huffed Magnus. "The witness is excused."

"Before I take m'leave," my colossal friend said, addressing the crowd, "I think ol' Walter here has proven that he means y'no harm. If y'want to continue this trial, that is surely your choice, but let a man have a decent seat, for cryin' out loud!"

Heads nodded all around us and Magnus mumbled, "I suppose." He nodded toward a battalion of soldiers, and I was freed of all my bonds.

There was a blur of motion as Paul's ax flew through the trees. In a matter of moments, he turned the timber into a proper chair for me. It felt good to sit.

Paul slapped me a high five, nodded to the crowd as they burst into applause, and strode off in the direction from which he came.

Magnus next spoke with authority. "I'm not certain, Walter, that your theatrics are doing you much good. You still haven't convinced me that, with few exceptions, giants are more than stupid and dangerous."

"Giants are smarter than you think, Magnus."

"More than I think, you say? This isn't about what I think. It's about facts."

"You know," I replied, "a friend of mine says, 'Never let the facts get in the way of the truth.' Let me tell you a story, and I think you'll see what I mean."

FINE! Go ahead and tell your story.

Once in my travels, searching for my giant relatives throughout the world, I came across a reference to a giant unknown to me: Atlas, King of Mauritania. Intrigued, I took a trip to North Africa in search of the fabled king.

My journey led me to a cave in the foothills of the mountains where an enormous cavern opened to reveal the heavens above. There, standing still as a statue, I found a giant nearly twice my size. He seemed as if in a trance, so I moved slowly into his line of sight. He made only a slight movement of his head, showing that he saw me, but nothing more. We stood staring at each other for a long time.

"What is it you want?" he finally asked.

"I am a storyteller and a giant, descended, I believe, from you and your kind. I have come to see if you were real."

"Real I am. Now go away."

I did not move.

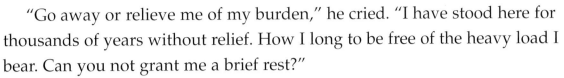

"Go away or relieve me of my burden," he cried. "I have stood here for thousands of years without relief. How I long to be free of the heavy load I bear. Can you not grant me a brief rest?"

"You really do hold up the heavens," I observed. "Did Zeus do this to you?"

"If you want to hear my story, you'll have to trade places with me," he said. "Here," he coaxed, "take it just for a minute."

"I don't think I'm big enough," I protested, but the Titan persisted.

"You'll adjust. It seems too big at first, but you get used to it."

"How do I do it?" I asked, still skeptical.

"Hold out your arms, such as I have done," he replied, his voice distinctly less weary. "I will lower mine. Thus will the burden be transferred."

I won't tell you it was easy, because it wasn't, but I wasn't crushed, as I had feared. I was holding up the heavens!

Atlas ripped the manacles from his hands and sat down for the first time in 6,000 years. Then he ripped the chains off his feet.

"You cannot know what relief I feel just now," he said, his voice brightening.

He smiled at me, a dazzling smile, full of gratitude.

I tried to be gracious and give him one in return, but my mind was more on my task than my manners. I did notice, however, that 6,000 years of hard physical labor and no bath had left Atlas smelling of a heady mix of sweat and ambrosia.

"Uh, Atlas," I offered, "you're kind of ripe."

He raised his left armpit and took a whiff. "Hoo! By my great father, Uranus, I see what you mean." He scooted away to a corner of the cavern and rested with his back against a wall.

I wondered how long he intended me to stand here like this. I was starting to sweat from the exertion, and not being a god, I didn't smell anything like ambrosia.

"So, I've given you your first break in thousands of years, huh?"

"Indeed, and I am very grateful," he said with a twinkle in his eye. Then he leaped up and was gone.

I was horrified. Atlas had abandoned me to do his job while he went off who knows where. Just great! I was feeling quite stupid for allowing myself to be tricked.

I was left to learn how to hold these heavens up without killing myself. Over the days and weeks I figured I could shift my weight slightly without losing my cargo.

Once my nose itched so badly I simply had to scratch it. I brought my hand to my face very slowly. And to my surprise, the heavens didn't come crashing down around me.

I lowered both hands slowly, to test my discovery. I felt the weight shift to my head and shoulders, but nothing happened. Then I had an idea! I slowly bent down on my hands and knees. The weight moved to the center of my back, as if I were giving the universe a horsey ride.

Then, I tucked my head to my chest and lifted my buttocks into the air. An amazing thing happened: the pressure of the heavens began to slide down my back to the ground, until they came off my back altogether.

I held my breath, waiting for some cosmic calamity, but there was none. The Earth was now supporting whatever I had been holding up with my body. I was free.

"Aren't you a clever one?" came a booming voice. It was Atlas, who had quietly returned. "I stood there for 6,000 years never once thinking the Earth could do the job instead of me. I'm a fool."

"It's good to see you, Atlas," I said. I was glad to see he had not planned to abandon me forever. I was also glad the heavens were off my back, and that I could go and take a bath. I was pretty stinky!

He reached down, grabbed me around the waist, and leaped out of the cave, landing on the highest peak in the mountain range. He set me down and then sat down next to me.

"There wasn't much for me out there, you know," he said wistfully. "The world I knew is long gone. And there really is no place for a giant anymore. Even to hold up the heavens.

"Even chained as I was, I knew I had a purpose in my life," he said as he gazed into the distance. "Holding up the heavens, though a punishment, was a job I took seriously.

"People who lived in this part of the world used to worship me. After a few centuries, though, they forgot about me."

He turned to look at me. "I thank you for my freedom, brother giant. Now it is time for me to sleep."

Atlas stretched out his huge legs into the valley below, then nestled his body between two mountains as neatly as if the space were made for him. He curled into a ball, gave me one last glance, and fell asleep. He had returned to his mother, Gaea, and she embraced him warmly as he faded from view and became part of the mountains that bear his name.

NONSENSE!

"That story is preposterous!" Magnus interjected. "Besides, you come across as easily duped. I don't think you are making the case that giants are smart!"

"Believe what you will, Magnus, but there are all kinds of giants, just as there are all kinds of people," I replied.

Suddenly there was a crashing in the distance, and the crowd of little people huddled together in fear. All eyes turned to Magnus, who held his hand to his lips and peered into the darkness, trying to find the source of the noise. Then he looked at me with confusion. If I was here, what could be making the noise?

At last, I knew what had been causing all the trouble on their island.

"Magnus," I called.

"*Shhhhh!*" he hissed. He waited a few more moments, then when he felt that the danger had passed, he resumed the trial as if nothing had happened. "If there is nothing more, I'd like to—"

"Wait!" I shouted. Magnus was never going to listen to me. I had to end this trial once and for all. "Giants are clever and work quite well with all people, even little ones."

"I suppose you have just the story?" said Magnus with a weary smile.

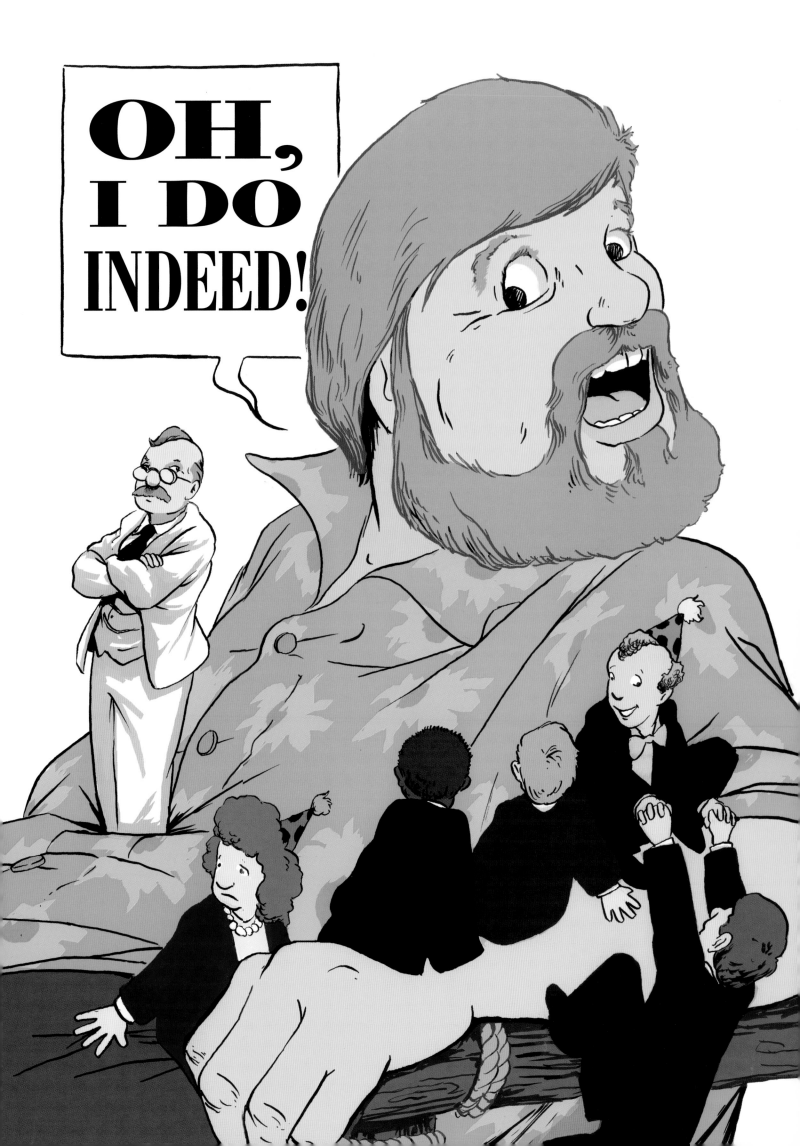

Finn saves the Giant Babies

And Defeats the Black Witch

(WITH THE HELP OF THE SMALL MEN)

Now, doubtless you've heard of Finn M'Cool, the greatest hero fair Ireland ever produced? Finn was a king, a warrior, a poet, and a learned man to boot. He was the largest of his race, and that, combined with all his other qualities, made him a natural leader. His people loved him and they told stories of his deeds long after he died.

One day, Finn received a letter with a heart-wrenching plea for help.

Twice now, on the very evening of my children's birth, each of my sons has been stolen by a thief so sly that he has made fools of our guards and vexed our most learned men. No matter what preparations were made to protect these precious newborn babies, this cunning bandit has evaded capture. My queen, wretched with grief over the loss of our babes, will soon bring forth another child. If we were to lose another baby, surely her heart—and mine—would break into a million pieces! I beseech you, the great Finn M'Cool, to come and stand guard over our child and keep the babe safe.

Sincerely,

Morgenthau

King of the Island of the Big Men

Finn could not ignore such a call for help. With his pack on his back, Finn headed straight to a nearby fishing village to find a boat and crew to help him thwart the baby thief. He soon spied a group of small men playing hurley on the sands.

"Good day," said Finn.

"Good day to yourself, Finn M'Cool," said the Small Men as one.

"Who are you?" asked Finn. "And what is your calling?"

"We each have a different skill," said the smallest of the Small Men. "I am called Lazy Back, for when I sit down there's no one in the world that can make me rise again."

"I'll see about that," replied the skeptical Finn. With a good, strong hold around the Small Man's waist, Finn pulled with all his might, but he could not stir the Small Man off his seat.

Finn turned back to the group and asked each Small Man his name and his special talent.

Hearing Ear could hear so much as a whisper from as far away as the Eastern world.

Three Sticks could make anything out of wood.

Knowing Man knew everything that was going to happen in every part of the world.

Far Feeler could feel an ivy leaf falling in the Eastern world.

Climber could climb any structure, even a wall made of glass.

Bowman was so skilled an archer he could hit one gnat in a swarm of them dancing in the air.

Taking Easy could steal anything without being noticed.

Three Sticks interested Finn greatly. "How long would it take you to make a ship for me?" he asked him.

"Well," he replied, " 'tis nothin' I haven't faced before. Make a circle of yourself, Finn M'Cool!"

As Finn began to turn around, Three Sticks picked up a piece of driftwood at his feet, threw it out into the sea, and by the time Finn was facing front again, there stood before him a beautiful ship.

"Now I need to sail to the Island of the Big Men, where I must perform a service for their king. If you will all accompany me as my crew, I will reward you handsomely."

"We will take service with you," said Lazy Back, "and we will guide you well, for there is no part of the Eastern world that we have not faced before."

The king was so overjoyed to see the great Finn M'Cool and his tiny crew that he ordered a huge feast be prepared to honor them. As they dined in the enormous banquet hall, the king revealed that his wife had given birth that very morning.

"I have given this matter much thought," said Finn, "and I have devised a plan. Ready your strongest chamber for the child and his two most trustworthy nurses. My men and I will stand guard over this most precious treasure. If the child is stolen, in spite of our best efforts, I will answer for it with my head."

That night, Finn, the eight Small Men, the two nurses, and the infant prince were locked inside a high tower room with but one door and a fireplace.

As soon as the door was sealed, Knowing Man turned to Finn and said, "You were foolish to offer your head as a price for our failure. I can see that the child will be stolen tonight, despite our best efforts."

"Well, if you know that much," sputtered Finn in exasperation, "you could give us a clue as to who the enemy is that we are facing."

"That I can," replied the seer. "It is the king's own sister! She is a powerful witch who has a long-simmering feud with her brother and now steals his children for revenge. Her magic makes her invisible, and no number of guards or locks will prevent her from coming down the chimney and snatching the child from his cradle."

"I'll not be beaten without a fight," pronounced Finn. "Far Feeler, stretch your feelings out and alert us when she nears the palace. Hearing Man, you listen for the slightest sound of her coming down the chimney. Lazy Back, you sit down in front of the fireplace and grab hold of her so tightly that she cannot retreat. Bowman, have your bow and arrow at the ready. The rest of us will stay alert and do what we can when the time comes."

Hours passed until, just after midnight, Far Feeler called out, "I feel the witch getting ready to leave her castle through the door in the roof. Her castle has no ordinary doors. Its walls are high and as slippery as glass."

And it was but a short time before Hearing Man whispered, "She is here. The guards cannot see her, for she has made herself invisible."

"Everyone on his guard," ordered Finn.

As every eye turned to the fireplace, the shimmering outline of a long, bony hand appeared through the flames, reaching toward the cradle. But Lazy Back was upon it as soon as it cleared the flames and sat down with such a hold on the arm that there was nothing the witch could do to free it. She pulled and tugged, and after much effort, the arm came out of its socket and fell down the chimney and into Lazy Back's lap.

Separated from the witch's body, the arm instantly lost its invisibility. As Lazy Back threw the arm away from the baby, Bowman pinned it to the wall with his arrow.

Astounded at the length and size of the arm, Finn and the Small Men turned away from their charge for but a moment. In that instant, they heard a noise that made every man's hand go to his weapon. Turning back, they saw that the cradle was empty, and the horrified, screaming nurses were pointing to the fireplace, where the witch had stretched down her other arm to snatch up the baby, quick as lightning.

"Well, there's your head!" exclaimed Knowing Man.

Finn paced about the chamber for a moment and then announced, "There's not a moment to lose. Quickly, we must return to our ship."

"Run away?" gasped the Small Men. It seemed a cowardly thing to do, but they followed Finn as quietly as possible, lest they alert the sentries.

They set sail as swiftly as possible. The Small Men were, to a man, ashamed of their retreat, but Finn showed no signs of remorse. Once at sea, Finn turned to them and said, "Now, Far Feeler, use your abilities to point us in the direction of the witch's castle. We shall rescue all three sons of the king! Then won't he be pleased enough to forgive our failure this night?"

The Small Men set themselves to their tasks, each feeling foolish for not trusting the brave Finn. During their journey, Finn and the Small Men perfected a rescue plan. When they reached the Eastern world, Climber, Taking Easy, Far Feeler, and Lazy Back set out for the castle, leaving Finn and the others to guard the ship.

Climber found the high glass walls of the witch's castle no hindrance. " 'Tis nothin' I haven't faced before," he boasted, and he was up the wall and over the top as quick as you please, carrying Taking Easy on his back.

Once at the top it was Taking Easy's turn. " 'Tis nothin' I haven't faced before," said he, as he climbed down into the castle, quiet as a cat, and lifted one of the king's sons into his arms. He climbed back up the wall and out the open door and gave the still-sleeping child to Climber, who took him down to their comrades at the foot of the castle walls. This they repeated until all three sons were safe in the arms of the Small Men and aboard ship.

They sailed off into a night that had become blustery of wind and roiling of wave.

"The witch is coming! I can hear her screams of rage," cried Hearing Ear.

"Bowman," yelled Finn, "we must prepare for the witch's attack. Shoot straight and we will not fail."

" 'Tis nothin' I haven't faced before!" roared Bowman. Upon first sight of the witch looming out of the blackness, he loosed on her an arrow that pierced the middle of her forehead, whereupon she fell dead into the sea.

When Finn and his crew returned to the Island of the Big Men with their priceless cargo, the king was jubilant. He ordered a feast to end all feasts in celebration of their heroic deeds. It lasted eight days and nights and was accompanied each day by a gift of gold, jewels, and riches for each of the Small Men. Finn accepted only a gold ring with the king's seal as a promise that should Finn ever require the assistance of anyone from the Island of the Big Men, it would be given without question.

On the ninth day, with their ship full of the king's bounty, Finn and the Small Men set sail for home.

"Quite an adventure, wouldn't you say?" Finn asked the Small Men. But he already knew what their answer would be . . .

" 'Tis nothin' we haven't faced before!"

Cheers erupted from the crowd. Clearly, the little people liked my story.

"Let him go, Magnus," came a small woman's voice. "He's not our enemy and he's made himself a strong case that giants aren't, either."

Magnus looked only slightly convinced. "Well . . ."

Then there was more noise in the distance. The crowd jumped as one. I heard a loud bark coming from the trees and decided to put an end to their fears.

"Barnabas!" I yelled, and gave a loud whistle.

Bounding out of the woods came my dog, playfully chasing a small herd of cows. Little people scattered and ran for cover as Barnabas, happy to see me, licked my face and forgot all about the animals.

"Sit, boy!" I commanded. Barnabas, ever cooperative, did so.

"This is Barnabas, everyone. He means no harm. But like me, he is often judged harshly due to his extreme size. He didn't mean to 'terrorize' your island, and if we can have your help in building a ship, we'll sail home and not bother you again."

Magnus emerged from the shadows and the hushed crowd followed him. "Very well. If you promise to take that beast away, we will assist you."

I stood up stiffly, every muscle aching.

"Dare I presume that the verdict is in my favor, Magnus?" I asked.

"Indeed you dare," was the reply from below. "You mean us no harm, that much is clear. It wouldn't be right to hold you accountable for the crimes of your ancestors."

More cheers from the crowd, though Barnabas's presence made them maintain a safe distance.

"Besides," he said, smiling, "we all enjoyed your stories. The verdict is not guilty!"

Notes on the Stories in This Book

Before I left the island, I wanted to give the little people some background on the stories I told them. Here's what I left them:

Stories were told, first and foremost, and retold until folks knew them by heart. It was a long time before anyone thought to set them down on paper, and then people often forgot where they heard a particular story in the first place. The earliest books of stories didn't give notes or sources, and few bothered with giving credit to other storytellers because stories belong to everyone and storytellers are always borrowing tales from each other.

Nowadays, it is just good manners to let your audience know where your stories come from and to give credit where credit is due.

JACK

My version of Jack isn't based on any one telling. I took the story everyone hears while growing up and tried to show the giant's side of the conflict.

PAUL

The story of Paul Bunyan's origin involves some controversy. Some say the version we all know was invented by W. B. Laughead, an advertising executive for the Red River Lumber Company, in 1922. But there are stories about a giant lumberjack dating to the last third of the nineteenth century throughout the American and Canadian wilderness. We'll never know, I guess, 'cause Paul refuses to tell us.

STORMY

Like Paul's, the versions of Ol' Stormalong's exploits are numerous. I found several dozen versions of a sea shanty about him, each with many verses. Paul's tale in this book is mostly based on a story from *Here's Audacity! American Legendary Heroes*, by Frank Shay (The Macaulay Company, 1930).

ATLAS

This is my own story, written to correct the notion that Atlas holds up the Earth, as is so often (and incorrectly) portrayed.

FINN

Most contemporary retellings of his exploits are based on *Irish Sagas and Folk-Tales*, retold by Eileen O'Faolain (H. Z. Walck, 1954). O'Faolain's Finn stories were based on "notes taken down from Irish-speaking storytellers in Kerry by Jeremiah Curtin toward the end of the nineteenth century." Her story "Finn, the Giants and the Small Men" is the basis for my Finn tale in this book.

You'll find a lot of information on various kinds of giants, including all of the other giants mentioned in my book, in a beautifully illustrated volume called *Giants*, illustrated by Julek Heller, Carolyn Scrace, and Juan Wijngaard; devised by David Larkin; text by Sarah Teale (H. N. Abrams, 1979).

A LIST OF MY FAVORITE BOOKS ABOUT GIANTS

Abiyoyo, by Pete Seeger, illustrations by Michael Hays, Simon & Schuster, 1986.

The BFG, by Roald Dahl, illustrations by Quentin Blake, Farrar, Straus & Giroux, 1982.

Big Men, Big Country, by Paul Robert Walker, illustrations by James Bernardin, Harcourt, 1993.

Delphine, by Molly Bang, Morrow, 1988.

Fin M'Coul, the Giant of Knockmany Hill, by Tomie dePaola, Holiday House, 1981.

The Giant, by Mordecai Gerstein, Hyperion, 1995.

Giants! Stories from Around the World, by Paul Robert Walker, illustrations by James Bernardin, Harcourt, 1995.

Golem, by David Wisniewski, Clarion, 1996.

Jack and the Seven Deadly Giants, by Sam Swope, illustrations by Carll Cneut, Farrar, Straus & Giroux, 2004.

Mangaboom, by Charlotte Pomerantz, illustrations by Anita Lobel, Greenwillow, 1997.

Sea Monster
Sea

Dark
Castle

Happy Giant Island

Lake Toothy

Boutie Outlet

Boutie Inlet

Giant Wave Oce

Land of
Big Bad Beasts

Blood Claw
Islands

Smooshed City

Bad Choice River